Table of Contents

Attributions

The cover and other images used in this work are by <u>Enrique Meseguer</u> and <u>Clker-Free-Vector-Images</u> from <u>Pixabay</u> and are used with permission.

Evocation

... in order that Satan might not outwit us.
For we are not unaware of his schemes.

2 Corinthians 2:11

Foreword

I have benefited much from reading C.S. Lewis' *Screwtape Letters*. Lewis' warnings on the dangers inherent in living the Christian life – sounded through the mouth of the devil Screwtape – were prophetic to his generation, and just as relevant today.

C.S. Lewis' imaginative framing for his *Screwtape Letters* is as entertaining as it is profound. It takes as its inspiration the inverse concept of a "guardian angel". If every saint had a guardian angel assigned by God to protect them, might not they also have a diabolical tempter assigned by the devil to lead them astray?

In a sense, Satan's schemes never change: the devil is always and forever out to "steal, kill and destroy" (John 10:10). On the other hand, the devil's snares do indeed change: in the sense that they are tailored to the present generation. In other words, as the worldview or mindset of the present generation differs from those that have gone before; Satan's deceits are adjusted accordingly - to ensnare all the more surely.

Satanic schemes – as described in the body of this work - are diabolically clever – but not altogether surprising. I am quite convinced from reading the emails in this collection that more will follow.

Readers interested in reading more original, creative works are invited to connect with me via the social media links provided via my website: antipodeanwriter.wordpress.com.

Antipodean Writer
Canberra, Australia
August 2020

Preface

I had tried repeatedly filtering all emails from "hell.org" to send them automatically to my spam folder but without success. These emails always seemed to evade whatever filters I put in place and land squarely in my inbox.

Frustrated, I contacted my sysadmin for help: only for him to eventually conclude there was nothing he could do. He told me that "hell.org" was not a registered domain and had no DNS record and therefore could not be blocked. By way of reply, I forwarded to him copies of some of the annoying emails I had received and asked him to do something about it. But the sysadmin has never got back to me.

Of course, I never intended to read these emails. But one day as I was methodically working my way through my inbox, an email arrived and I opened it automatically. It was another email from "hell.org", and contained directions from an executive to a junior staff member to implement certain directives – which interested readers can read for themselves.

There is no earthly reason for such emails to arrive in my inbox. Whether there is some anomalous quantum flux in the hell dimensions that misdirects such emails to me – or some other reason – I shall probably never know.

Regardless, I publish this collection of emails to forewarn the saints and allow them to become forearmed against the devil and his current schemes.

Antipodean Writer

When Darkness Falls

*Intercepted emails from an Executive Devil
to a Junior Tempter*

Antipodean Writer

Fellowship Free Zones

From: \<Weasel\> weasel@hell.org
To: \<Skunk\> skunk@hell.org
Subject: Fellowship Free Zones

Skunk,

How many times have I reminded you that none of your line-managers give a fig about whether or not your patient attends church. That your patient has started attending a local church is not the end of the world – or not yet, anyway. And you most certainly cannot blame this circumstance for your latest deplorable grading.

You should know by now that local churches, these days, are so much putty in our hands: they can be reshaped virtually as we will. In which case, you should be getting on with creating inside your patient's local church a *Fellowship Free Zone*.

Setting up a Fellowship Free Zone, old boy, is frightfully simple. Your aim, obviously, is to guarantee that whenever your patient attends church he finds himself a solitary, isolated individual floating in a sea of gormless apathy. When the Saints unite, we are forced to retreat (or end up inside the nearest herd of swine): but isolated and alone, church-goers make for easy pickings. To ensure your patient stays isolated, you must get your own hands dirty – this is no time for shirking!

Allow me to make some suggestions to ensure that your Fellowship Free Zones function as intended:

1. **Busy-ness.** (Surely the easiest strategy!) Keep every church volunteer so overwhelmed with multitudinous activities they are too busy to talk to newcomers. Newcomers must "fend for themselves", which means that they invariably end up staring haplessly at blank walls in embarrassed silence pretending to wait for a friend. Few newcomers – if any – will repeat the experience: one such Sunday morning is usually enough to convince them never to return.

2. **Greeting Team Members.** Fill church Greeting Teams with introverts: who will burn out quickly and become resentful at ever being rostered on at all. This is so simple to arrange – and so amusing to watch from the sidelines!

   With extroverts you must use greater finesse to negate all their efforts. Usually the best method is distraction: divide their attention between so many people that they only manage to share some few words each, and never get to really impact or effectively encourage anyone. Pretend to the extrovert that such a momentary acquaintanceship is meaningful: whereas we both know quite well that the opposite is invariably the case. Shallow acquaintanceships are almost quite as effective at preventing genuine fellowship as avoiding church entirely in the first place.

3. **Hypocrisy.** For those few, extraordinary patients who cannot take a hint – and there are always one or two – a final step might be necessary. It is simply this: be careful to continually point out to your patient the blatant hypocrisy of the church-members he comes into contact with. It is simple matter to show him that (for example) Greeting Team members will only ever speak to him when they are rostered to do so: and that these same people either avoid or ignore him the rest of the time. Once you get your patient to realise this – how long will it take before he loses interest in attending church altogether?

In short, there is really nothing to it. Put these tried-and-true strategies into practice and your progress to Tempter Base Grade 2 is assured.

I look forward to your next field-report with anticipation.

Weasel.

Executive Director
Probation and Ongoing Training
Trainee Tempter Education Directorate

Virtual Fellowship

From: <Weasel> weasel@hell.org
To: <Skunk> skunk@hell.org
Subject: Virtual Fellowship

Skunk,

I have read with interest your report on the advantages of using social media, and look forward to your further researches into this topic. Some of your points I took to be especially suggestive of fruitful endeavours for our field-agents: and these I enumerate below.

As we labour to provide virtual reality substitutes for the real thing, we will soon be able to easily isolate individuals from each other. Individual Saints are always far easier to manipulate than groupings of the same. (Our master forfend the Saints actually come together in person and become the Body of Christ!)

1. **Promote virtual friendships.** From past experience we know only too well the dangers of real friendships springing up between two saints. Happily for us, you correctly identify that such dangers can be deftly avoided by encouraging our patients to seek out "virtual friends". (What delightful self-deception!) "Virtual friends", of course, are not friends at all in any meaningful sense of the term: they are ersatz individuals who endure you only as long you consume negligible amounts of their time, effort, and money.

Which is why virtual friends are perfect for our purposes. Our patients can be easily sold the idea that virtual friendships are efficient and convenient: after all, you can text them "anywhere, anytime, 24x7". Reinforce this specious reasoning with the mantra that "texting is every bit as good as talking": a statement so palpably false that only humans could believe it. Texting, as you point out, is really designed for vacuous and facile messaging: a vehicle for pithy but perfectly meaningless platitudes. (LOL!)

The rather obvious truth that even ten thousand texts will never equal even a single conversation in person must be concealed from our patients at all costs. Additionally, we must never even hint that their carefully-curated virtual identities are simply a mask for the patient to hide behind: as they are too lazy or too afraid to genuinely open up. If any patient should discover symptoms of wanting to actually talk openly with another: smother the impulse with temptations to choose comfortable seclusion and the most "efficient" use of their time.

2. **Promote virtual churches.** It follows from the first point that virtual groups of all kinds – virtual bible studies, virtual worship, virtual churches – have great potential. By all means, seek to develop these ideas further. Perhaps you could launch a few pilot projects in western nations, before selecting the best-performers for replication worldwide? Patients could login to their own myChurch dashboard, select their personalised worship-songs, and stream their favourite audio-sermon: all without ever leaving the comfort of home!

Weasel.

Executive Director
Probation and Ongoing Training
Trainee Tempter Education Directorate

Prayer Meetings

From: <Weasel> weasel@hell.org
To: <Skunk> skunk@hell.org
Subject: Prayer Meetings

Skunk,

Your concerns are overblown about your patient attending prayer meetings at his local church. This is hardly a matter for concern: indeed, it has been well-known throughout our infernal regions for years that "prayer meetings" for the greatest part consist of no prayer at all – at least, only prayer that is misdirected, misinformed, and consequently ineffectual. So great and so effective have been the labour of our best propagandists over these last years: I should be surprised if a single patient present knew anything about praying at all.

In the unlikely circumstance that the assembled patients do pray – we have only to remember the words of our Enemy: "the prayers of a righteous man avail much", and therefore the prayers of a distracted, easily upset nincompoop avail little or nothing. Remember the low calibre of your patient, and take heart. Who among them still believes in miracles these days?

However, you are quite right to take precautions against the unexpected wiles of the Enemy. By concerting your efforts with Grubnat – who, I recall, is in charge of the local minister – you will be easily able to cultivate a perfect den of iniquity inside your particular prayer-meeting.

Simply start applying any of the following remedies:

→ **Distraction.** Drop the occasional thought into a patient's mind about all the things he must do tomorrow: always exaggerating the importance of the urgent and the trivial. Your starting point can be as simple as how uncomfortable his chair is: and then take it from there.

→ **Gossip.** Dress up ordinary gossip as "prayer requests". Stimulate the patient's curiosity to know all about what never concerns him in the least: humans always have a weakness to rejoice over the failings of others. For the best results – insinuate a little slander: implying the incompetence, malfeasance, stupidity, or whatever you like – of various church members. We all enjoy this kind of work: but don't press too hard at first. The best fruits take time to mature.

→ **Dissension.** This follows easily from the proceeding: simply point out to your patient – in as lurid colours as you can – how wrong-headed the others are. Raise fears in him about what is being said about himself behind his back: just as he been doing to others, won't those others be doing to him? This becomes such a fertile ground for sowing guilt – but we will discuss this another time.

The precise needs of the moment must determine your best course. I have no doubt as to your abilities to negate entirely the potential for any foothold of the Enemy to take root inside this particular prayer meeting.

Weasel.

Executive Director
Probation and Ongoing Training
Trainee Tempter Education Directorate

Small Groups

From: <Weasel> weasel@hell.org
To: <Skunk> skunk@hell.org
Subject: Small Groups

Skunk,

How many times must I remind you to remain cool when your patient takes a turn for the worse? Time is our ally here, as always. Other opportunities will appear down the road.

I have read your latest report closely – and I cannot see any reason for undue concern.

Your patient has started attending a mid-week bible-study. So – what of it? Your last report contained so much hyperbole that the facts were obscured. How can your patient possibly be falling into the hands of another "apostle Paul"? Balderdash! An enemy servant of the apostle Paul's caliber (one of our tragic failures – a much higher-ranked tempter should have been assigned to that one) arises but once in a millennium, thankfully. If you persist in writing me such fictions, I will see you transferred to Propaganda.

To return to the point: all bible-study groups (at least, those to which I was ever assigned) are easily diverted to serve our own purposes most admirably. We spend much effort in ensuring that plenty of pagans attend such groups – which is most useful to us: particularly when they lead the group.

Pull yourself together and follow any of the following suggestions – adding whatever else your own ingenuity suggests:

→ **Preaching without practice.** Let them read the bible as much as they wish. Encourage endless discussion about what it means. Avoid definite conclusions about anything. Encourage doubt as to whether the true meaning can ever be known.

Such bible-reading need cause no harm: do not we ourselves know their Scriptures by heart? Just so long as they never put what they read into practice, what Good can possibly come of it?

→ **Disarm prayer.** If prayer cannot be altogether avoided, disrupt it and make it ineffectual. Do not – I abjure you! – under any circumstances let them come to full-minded agreement when they pray. Even novice prayers cause us endless mischief when made in earnest. (It is most unfair how the Enemy stacks the field against us!) Therefore, use means to prevent two saints agreeing on anything – insert into their minds thoughts like: the (fallacious) need to finish on time, worry about (any cause will do), embarrassment over praying aloud (surprisingly effective), and so on.

→ **Criticism.** Disrupting unity to prevent fellowship is easy when attendees criticise each other. Focus on their differences, no matter how small or non-existent, in: speech, dress, income, age, background, or whatever. A well-placed criticism by one will spark quick defensiveness in the rest – shattering all incipient feelings of community. With a little good management you can easily provoke others to join in the criticism – and then expand the scope to encompass anyone not present. Few things prove more enjoyable than directing matters to this end.

→ **Gossip & Slander.** When a spirit of criticism is being established, adding gossip and slander to the mix is simplicity itself. Use some insinuations to get a foothold. As soon as slander and gossip start to operate – they quickly displace all other discussions and take on an infernal life of their own: as you well know. As easy as setting gasoline on fire!

→ **Selected Persecution.** To spice things up a bit, take the time to pick on one member for special attention. You will need to foster a decent group-mentality in the rest to precipitate a good bout of group-persecution: but this is usually child's play with weak-willed humans. Do your work properly and the persecutors will develop a delectable sense of self-righteous bigotry, while you simultaneously cultivate feelings of overwhelming despair or angry revenge (it matters little) in the one persecuted. The fruit of such labours is its own reward.

→ **Targeted Rejection.** Used hand in hand with any of the above: rejection has always been our strongest weapon. Wield the fear of rejection to negate all possibility of unity. By this means you may inculcate a wholesome 'fear of man' inside each group member: and members desperate to conform will do anything they are told to do, and thus become useful tools for our own purposes.

It matters nothing whether your own patient is on the giving or the receiving end of any of the above strategies: we win gloriously either way. Letting no opportunity pass, and success is assured.

Weasel.

Executive Director
Probation and Ongoing Training
Trainee Tempter Education Directorate

Public Apologies

From: <Weasel> weasel@hell.org
To: <Skunk> skunk@hell.org
Subject: Public Apologies

Skunk,

Public Apologies are one of our newest and most useful tools in deluding the current generation of patients. A modicum of subtlety is required – which you demonstrate on your better days – for optimal results. You have already been taught the basics: now is the time for you to get your patient to practice this most useful activity.

However, as your mentor, I must mention a few points which cannot be too often repeated.

1. **First:** never forget that your patient must confess loudly the sins of others – but *not his own*. Confessing the sins of others is a congenial pass-time leading to the rapid growth of complacent pride: which is most useful to us. Confessing one's own sins puts the patient in deadly peril – for it opens a route to humility and the possibility of real repentance. Happily for us, keeping your patient focused on pointing out the sins of others is an easy matter: just be sure he daily checks his social media and news feeds – which our agents continually update with the most violent, salacious, and titillating stories possible. Remember: the log in your patient's eye is always best used to beat others over the head with.

2. **Second:** ensure your patient starts making false public apologies into a habit. This should be easy enough: because denouncing others allows every patient to feel good about themselves – while simultaneously avoiding any of the personal sacrifices that accompany really being Good. Remind your patient of the joys of occupying the moral high ground - which is part and parcel of confessing the sins of others - and stress continually the pain which accompanies confessing one's *own* sins. Remember to emphasise that "pain is always evil" (and must therefore be avoided): which will ensure your patient continues to be properly motivated.

3. **Third:** ensure your patient expresses their false public apologies to as many as possible, in as many different fora as possible, as loudly as possible, for as long as possible. Teach him that "a virtuous person is not one who actually practices virtue – but *one who expresses the correct viewpoint*", and therefore the most virtuous person expresses the correct view the most loudly and most often.

You must be careful to avoid anything that might spur the patient to action: patients who begin acting virtuously have been known to trigger The Enemy's deadliest weapon – Grace – against which we are helpless. But nothing ventured, nothing gained! And we can take considerable comfort from most patients' natural aversion to positive action of any kind. With our help, every patient will embrace our motto of "more talk – less action"!

4. **Finally:** cultivate your patient's comfortable feeling of self-satisfaction. False public apologies naturally lead the patient to expressing themselves in terms of grandiose, unctuous moralizing. Encourage such sentiments by every means at your disposal: for self-satisfied patients rarely – if ever – bother taking concrete action of any kind. Your patient should, by this stage, feel in high spirits for having exposed the sins of others: which lesson is reinforced whenever you helpfully remind him of his own shame should his own faults ever be similarly exposed. Hypocrisy is such a wonderful tool in our trade!

I trust that you will apply my suggestions assiduously and dutifully. If you do, your patient's presumptuous pride cannot but flourish – and so, in time, we may safely usher him to a warm welcome in our Father's House.

Weasel.

Executive Director
Probation and Ongoing Training
Trainee Tempter Education Directorate

Homosexuality

From: <Weasel> weasel@hell.org
To: <Skunk> skunk@hell.org
Subject: Homosexuality

Skunk,

You asked me to expand my reasons for thinking church attendance – at the right kind of church, of course – quite harmless. For the present let me limit myself to the most successful of our recent propaganda efforts: the promotion of homosexuality from the pulpit.

For years we have been busily inserting our own pastors and priests inside churches of every denomination. Our best operatives possess infinitely pliable moral fibre to make them exquisitely susceptible to every change in public opinion: and unable to resist whatever tendencies are trending in society at large. Therefore if society affirms homosexuality – so will they. It is, as they say, "a given".

Hand-in-hand with our continuing Pastor Insertion Program, we are actively reshaping society to destroy that most hateful institution of the Enemy's – the nuclear family. Our allies, the radical feminists – hating all male authority figures impartially – continue promoting our own anti-procreation / anti-marriage agenda and offer lesbian alternatives to pervert female libido. We coordinate their efforts with our pro-homosexual agitators: who inundate society with pseudo-scientific mumbo-jumbo and various social-theories to divide and confuse our opponents. Some examples of their work include: "Gender Identity

Syndrome", and "masculinity / femininity are social constructs" – to name but two.

Subverting truth is not merely pleasurable: it has its serious side also. Co-opting our patients' logic – that bizarre, human cognitive faculty – we convince them to accept its extreme conclusions. In the present case: authority figures constantly re-iterate that "men are no different from women". Once our patients come to believe this, it is a simple step to convince them – logically – that it matters nothing whether they next sleep with a man or woman: for there's "no difference", is there? And from homosexual sex it is a baby step to lead the patient to endorse homosexual marriage. Q.E.D.

Such thinking errors always compound: in this instance, by preventing nuclear families from ever coming into existence in the first place. Our patients instead accept our palliatives of barren, libidinous, multiple sexual-partners that are changed frequently in their unending pursuit of novelty over intimacy. Thus we unwind the Enemy's plans unveiled first in Eden – just as our master has directed.

Meantime, our double-agents within the church perform their role to perfection by confirming that heterosexual marriage is redefined out of legal existence. You express your worry that attending church might allow your patient to inadvertently learn some real biblical truth: but your concerns are grossly exaggerated. You evidently forget that our priests and pastors long ago rejected all Biblical authority whatever. If our double-agents actually open the Bible at all – to them it is a dead book: an error-riddled narrative of mythological fairy-tales requiring extensive reinterpretation. Their thin veneer of righteousness has no Power at all – certainly none to harm us. And thus they continue faithfully proclaiming "homosexual marriage" propaganda from their pulpits, and brazenly denouncing anyone teaching that "the Bible condemns homosexuality" as sinful.

But that's enough for now of this diverting topic. Do write and tell me how your current patient is coming along.

Weasel.

Executive Director
Probation and Ongoing Training
Trainee Tempter Education Directorate

Church Attendance

From: <Weasel> weasel@hell.org
To: <Skunk> skunk@hell.org
Subject: Church Attendance

Skunk,

It is regrettable that your patient is still attending church services on Sundays. Still, it is foolish to lose heart over such an unimportant setback – when so many things are still in our favour.

For instance: due to our hard work inside theological seminaries over past decades, there are fewer and fewer Christians today behind the pulpit on a given Sunday in any given denomination. Seminary institutions graduate for us every year a terrific batch of pantheists, agnostics, and atheists: subsidised by the churches themselves! Once installed, our non-Christian pastors commence teaching our own doctrines of unbelief: using their pulpit-given authority to undermine the Enemy's cause by promoting whatever we think best suits the times.

So I need hardly write how important it is to direct your patient to attend such a church. I have it on good authority that there are several excellent alternatives conveniently situated in your immediate area – so see to it that you draw your patient's attention to one of these. Speak to Grubnat for further details.

You write that inside a church – any church – untold dangers await to trap your patient in the most unavoidable errors. Do you think we are unaware of this? Hardly! It has long been well known among us that even lay-people may, from time to time, exercise the most pernicious influence. Indeed, the Enemy maliciously delights in raising up the unlikeliest specimens to do us untold damage – at precisely the moment when things are running most smoothly. This danger – you are correct in maintaining – is ever-present.

But do not over-exaggerate the risks: for these have been moderated considerably by our indefatigable exertions. Against all odds, our agents have so eroded the practice of instructing new believers that many church congregations today have few or no Christians in them at all. And we perpetuate this wonderful state of affairs – as you have already guessed – by pumping out incessant good-feeling pulpit propaganda to keep them lulled into a soporific sense of false security: the feeling that they are "saved" when, of course, they never were.

Select any of these false Christians – or neo-pagans, as I prefer to call them – for your patient's companions: they will themselves encourage him to avoid any harmful pursuits. For example: they can instruct your patient on how best to improve his self-esteem – or some other harmless diversion. They might also convince him – as most church-goers today fervently believe – that all shame is deeply sinful. Once our patients believe this they become more immune to being convicted about their own wrongdoing – and therefore give up trying to change anything about themselves. Which is exactly the way we want them.

You have before you abundant examples, case studies, and materials to work with: select what suits your patient's particular circumstances and improvise from there.

We can expand upon these themes at another time.

Weasel.

Executive Director
Probation and Ongoing Training
Trainee Tempter Education Directorate

The Great Divorce

From: <Weasel> weasel@hell.org
To: <Skunk> skunk@hell.org
Subject: The Great Divorce

Skunk,

To us who have for so long been enjoying the reliable and fruitful harvests of the divorce industry, can it really be true, that you – of all tempters! - have overlooked the advantages divorcees provide us with as they intermingle with a given church congregation? I cannot quite believe it!

Still, I am mortified to think that you have obviously yet to master such a basic lesson. And master it you must - if you wish to attempt our master's more subtle stratagems. As I always say, a good tempter must become brilliant at the basics! So pay close attention to what I write, and you will no doubt learn something to your advantage.

If you had been concentrating at lectures, you would already know that every church congregation is home to a quantity of divorcees: a goodly number of divorced women with a sprinkling of divorced men. You must not, for a moment, overlook these poor, hurting souls! They represent for us a gift-wrapped opportunity: so, seize the day!

It is clear to me from your latest (deplorable) field progress report that you desperately need someone to give you a few pointers. Therefore, take these suggestions from an old master-hand.

Your Goal: craft different strategies to target men and women. Men and women are different, you young fool! Generic temptations go oft astray, and are, anyway, at best half-realised. You must get to know your audience. Can it possibly have escaped your notice that divorced women tend to clump together for mutual self-expression, while divorced men prefer burying their hurt deep inside? Both responses present us with opportunities: but - as I said above - you need to create different strategies to maximise our harvest.

→ **For divorced women:** encourage these to meet together for "support". Start up a church "Support Group for Divorced Women" or similar. Next, encourage the women who attend to express their rancour openly - let them blame their ex-husband for all of their current problems. Their group motto must be: *Never accept responsibility – nothing was ever my fault!*

From such simple beginnings you can gently guide the entire group to revel in festering bitterness, which soon blooms into fully-fledged unforgiveness. Encourage these women to question, "Why did God do this to me?". Blaming God is always the best target for our patients' resentment, allowing them a prolonged wallowing in misery as they severally recall the details of every past wrong suffered (real or imagined – it makes no difference to us!). By keeping these women securely chained to the rotting corpse of past misdeeds, we pre-emptively prevent any chance that the Enemy might act to heal them. Now we have them right where we want them!

→ **For divorced men:** encourage these to "be strong and soldier on" - alone, without even a single, genuine friend to turn to for support or counsel. Most men default to this behaviour anyway: but for the rest you should shower them liberally with discouragement from uncaring acquaintances - who shrug apathetically whenever an attempt to express honest feelings.

Be diligent in encouraging mens' self-isolation by providing plenty of passive entertainment – games, movies, TV serials, downloadable apps, etc. – to give them enough time to slowly harden their hearts into stone.

Help things along by allowing such men to experience the full disapproval of other church members: this will allow them to perceive that the church is prejudiced against them and holds them fully responsible for their marriage-failure. (Which, of course, many churches do!) Such accusations, carefully nursed, can blossom into a beautiful harvest of bitterness and / or guilt: either outcome is most useful to us. The idea is to blind your patients to anything Good, allowing us to lead them without resistance down successive paths of despair to lodge finally in our father's house.

These strategies are so basic and easy to implement that even you shouldn't be able to mess them up. Follow my suggestions above and I have little doubt that your grades will rapidly improve.

Weasel.

Executive Director
Probation and Ongoing Training
Trainee Tempter Education Directorate

Your Best Life Now

From: <Weasel> weasel@hell.org
To: <Skunk> skunk@hell.org
Subject: Your Best Life Now

Skunk,

It is with considerable amusement that I read about your latest initiative: guiding the senior pastor under your care to adopt a slew of worldly management slogans to grow his church. You have obviously been paying attention to my instruction: I am proud of you. With your charge's growing reliance upon worldly wisdom, the Spirit of the Enemy will be increasingly constrained: and you will soon have the entire church under your direction.

Adopting a trendy catchphrase "Your Best Life Now" as your church's marketing and advertising banner was an inspired choice: worthy of comparison with the achievements of your illustrious ancestors - such as myself. Frequent recourse to, and repetition of, the mantra "Your Best Life Now" will do much to obscure and lead seekers away from the Enemy's Gospel.

Emphasise to your patient he must avoid anything "negative" in his preaching. Never mention "sin" – such a terribly negative and depressing subject! – or topics such as "atonement", "divine wrath", or "substitution". With careful and attentive management you will ensure that the Enemy's Gospel message is quietly laid aside, whilst your pastor wastes his efforts "being positive".

One of the delightful advantages of the "Your Best Life Now" slogan is that it is entirely false: only the biblically illiterate could possibly believe it. But pastors and their congregations today are, for the most part, just that – biblically illiterate! Your role is to perpetuate this wonderful status quo. To that end, I enclose the following suggestions:

1. Celebrate Everything, Condemn Nothing. Condemnation is so *negative* – even condemning sin! Therefore, as I mentioned above, your patient must never even mention such subjects. When church-goers ask irritating questions such as "Is gay marriage sinful?" – evade the question with pious-sounding platitudes. Instruct your patient to celebrate virtue (not holiness – more on this later) by selecting any of the unbiblical virtues so popular in the mainstream community, like "tolerance".

We might even take a biblical example, "marriage". Even here it is easy enough to corrupt something the Enemy created as good into its opposite. As "marriage" is extolled in the bible, your patient is already predisposed to celebrate it. That's all well and good, providing you extend the pastor to equally celebrate "gay marriage". Do this, and you have opened another broad, easy road to our father's house.

But I hear you protesting that your patient is not yet ready for such a step. Very well, bring to him couples getting married for the second, third, fourth, and fifth times – and insist he publicly celebrate these marriages also. Even better – get a divorced pastor to recite with the bride and groom vows of "lifelong fidelity". (The irony is delectable, is it not?) What better way exists to undermine our Enemy's design?

Surely our motive is clear? Celebrating a remarriage sanctions and endorses divorce: the one necessitates the other. Every remarriage defies the Enemy's teaching that "he (or she) who remarries commits adultery": and secures for our patients their greater condemnation. And condemnation carries with it such a delicious aroma of brimstone, don't you think?

2. False Gospels. Your patient has a terrific opportunity every week in the pulpit to spread our message – don't waste this opportunity. I suggest bringing to your patient's attention the "Prosperity Gospel" – one of our more popular alternatives.

A successful Prosperity Gospel message contains nothing negative (see above). Your pastor must emphasise that being materially poor, and all suffering, is always *bad*. The easiest way to do this is to make your pastor focus exclusively on the blessings of "wealth", "abundance" and "overflow". The not-so-subtle message is that all the poor and suffering are therefore cursed by God. What a fruitful opening for despair!

But there's more: a useful corollary to the Prosperity Gospel can be used to pervert the prayer-life of the whole congregation. It is this: have the pastor preach the message that "answered prayers" mean only prayers whereby the person asking gets what they wanted. The pastor's ready explanation for all "unanswered prayers" must be the petitioner's own lack of faith. Your patient must really come to believe that spiritual pygmies have unanswered prayers, whereas spiritual heroes get whatever they ask for when they pray each time, every time. Our goal is to reduce their God into a divine lolly-machine, dispensing goodies for every "right" prayer. Such delectable falsehoods will produce a rich harvest of discouragement, convincing many to walk away from church (and God) altogether.

This principle can be extended to make other Bible promises unconditional, thereby turning their God into a deity contracted to deliver a church-goer's demands. The Enemy is quickly reduced to being only a means to an end, such as to provide: more wealth, better health, or happy children. When the Enemy doesn't deliver, your patients can be encouraged to jettison Him for not keeping His end of the bargain. It is no matter that God never promised what they thought He did – your patients' ignorance is our opportunity! Derailing biblically-illiterate church-goers is so easy: it is like shooting fish in a proverbial barrel. They so easily become disillusioned, or retreat into increasingly frantic denials of reality to maintain a fragile pretense of faith.

We might explore these other issues more fully on a future occasion, for you have plenty to be going with as it is.

Weasel.

Executive Director
Probation and Ongoing Training
Trainee Tempter Education Directorate

A Short Note

From: <Weasel> weasel@hell.org
To: <Skunk> skunk@hell.org
Subject: A Short Note

Skunk,

I note with acute embarrassment your recent peevish and ill-considered complaints made to your supervisor regarding supposed difficulties with your present assignment. Your childish mewling is quite demeaning, yet this fails to stop you publicly lamenting your hard lot.

I am writing to you to say plainly that: of course your patient will have difficult moments. Have I now "felt your pain", dear boy?

That is about as much silly pop-psychology poppycock as I can manage: for when I was your age, we tempters had to work 24×7 shifts with multiple patients and never gave it a second thought. How degenerate your generation has become! When will you grow up? Earning a living isn't all fun and games, you dissipated demon! When will you and your friends ever come to the realise that life isn't one long party toting pitchforks while tormenting roomfuls of shrieking souls?

In point of fact, young devils like you have never had it so good. What has become painfully clear is your ingratitude – despite all of your generation's advantages. How I really do despair of today's young tempters! Your supervisor tells me he receives from you an endless stream of complaints – but never once any acknowledgement that your successes (pitiful as they are) are the inevitable fruit of seeds carefully sown by your wiser elders over past decades.

→ **Gay Marriage.** Allow me to make my point: for it is *my* generation who worked hard to turn the largest western Protestant denominations into publicly supporting Gay Marriage and sodomite sex (a great joke against their church founders!). It was *our* efforts that trained modern ministers of religion into beings so pliable that they now vociferously propound every false doctrine we care to suggest: so incapable have they become to discerning Truth from Falsehood!

→ **Public Education.** I might add – with becoming pride – that it is due to *my* generation that western Public Education now denigrates and denounces western culture, institutions, and history; substituting for the classics bowdlerised texts and works of revisionist writers that are as empty of facts as they are replete with politically-correct platitudes.

→ **Mainstream Media.** And *whose* generation was it who infiltrated global public newscasters and turned them into the effective propaganda machine they are today? (It always raises a laugh in hell when we hear their latest denunciations of "fake news"! With what delightful hypocrisy, what brazen effrontery, do these news-giants castigate everyone outside themselves!) It is no empty boast for me to say that we have recruited so many willing humans to distribute our propaganda material that our own PR department is becoming quite redundant.

→ **Western Islam.** Nor can I refrain from mentioning *our* latest signal success: badgering western governments into sponsoring and promoting Islam, to such an extent they pass "hate-speech" laws to silence their own citizens who criticise Islam publicly! The West today is more intolerant and less open than it was during the Middle Ages! (How quickly these humans forget history! Inveighing against religion was once a public freedom – now it is "religious vilification"! Ha! Ha!)

If you have been paying attention, you cannot fail to realise that with so many of your elders' schemes in play – after all your predecessors have done to smooth your path – you have nothing whatever to complain of. Indeed, nothing you have yet encountered with your patient is anything more than a trifling obstacle. Words fail me when I wonder whether your present generation is anything more than a pathetic bunch of second-rate, sniveling fiends.

Frankly, you need toughening up. Perhaps a spell of re-education on a remote, desert island inside a few wild pigs will do the trick? (Well, perhaps I would not go quite so far as all that: it is with a shudder I recall that most deplorable episode when the Enemy imprisoned some of our best field agents inside a herd of swine during their Galilean field assignment. What a fiasco!)

Anyhow, now that you have come up against your patient's token resistance – what are you going to do? Just give up – when you still have so many options left to choose from? My dear boy – you have all the tools to hand to reclaim your patient's attention and keep it fixed firmly upon temporal things. Modern social-media keeps humans glued to touch-screens all day long, everyday – leaving not a second's attention to attend to whatever the Enemy might say. If you do you job properly, as you were trained to do, you will soon have your patient back in hand.

I have no time to listen to your bleating that "the playing field is stacked against you", or how "the universe is so grossly unfair", or how "the Enemy might do something at any moment". Your protests are true – but irrelevant.

The real question is: are you to remain a spineless, carping, little fiend – or will you do your duty, stick to your patient through thick and thin, to at last escort him in triumph to our father's house?

Having read all that I have penned, I am confident that you will make the correct decision.

Weasel.

Executive Director
Probation and Ongoing Training
Trainee Tempter Education Directorate